ASTERIX AND THE GOTHS

TEXT BY GOSCINNY

DRAWINGS BY UDERZO

TRANSLATED BY ANTHEA BELL AND DEREK HOCKRIDGE

DARGAUD PUBLISHING INTERNATIONAL, LTD.

© DARGAUD EDITEUR PARIS 1963
© HODDER & STOUGHTON LTD. 1974
for the English language text

ISBN 0-917201-54-X

Exclusive licenced distributor for USA:

Distribooks Inc.
8220 N. Christiana Ave.
Skokie, IL 60076-2911
Tel: (708) 676-1596
Fax: (708) 676-1195
Toll-free fax: 800-433-9229

Imprimé en France-Publiphotoffset 93500 Pantin-en mars 1995

Printed in France

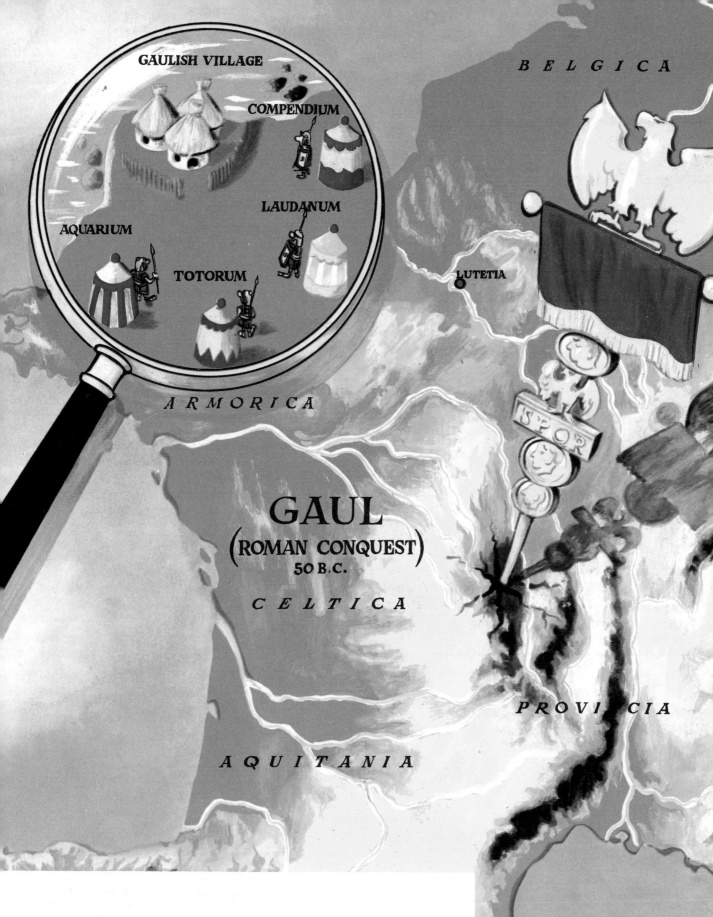

GAUL

(ROMAN CONQUEST)

50 B.C.

BELGICA

LUTETIA

CELTICA

PROVINCIA

AQUITANIA

ARMORICA

GAULISH VILLAGE

COMPENDIUM

LAUDANUM

AQUARIUM

TOTORUM

The year is 50 BC. Gaul is entirely occupied by the Romans.
Well, not entirely… One small village of indomitable Gauls still
holds out against the invaders. And life is not easy for the
Roman legionaries who garrison the fortified camps of
Totorum, Aquarium, Laudanum and Compendium…

a few of the Gauls ...

Asterix, the hero of these adventures. A shrewd, cunning little warrior; all perilous missions are immediately entrusted to him. Asterix gets his superhuman strength from the magic potion brewed by the druid Getafix...

Obelix, Asterix's inseparable friend. A menhir delivery-man by trade; addicted to wild boar. Obelix is always ready to drop everything and go off on a new adventure with Asterix — so long as there's wild boar to eat, and plenty of fighting.

Getafix, the venerable village druid. Gathers mistletoe and brews magic potions. His speciality is the potion which gives the drinker superhuman strength. But Getafix also has other recipes up his sleeve...

Cacofonix, the bard. Opinion is divided as to his musical gifts. Cacofonix thinks he's a genius. Everyone else thinks he's unspeakable. But so long as he doesn't speak, let alone sing, everybody likes him...

Finally, Vitalstatistix, the chief of the tribe. Majestic, brave and hot-tempered, the old warrior is respected by his men and feared by his enemies. Vitalstatistix himself has only one fear; he is afraid the sky may fall on his head tomorrow. But as he always says, 'Tomorrow never comes.

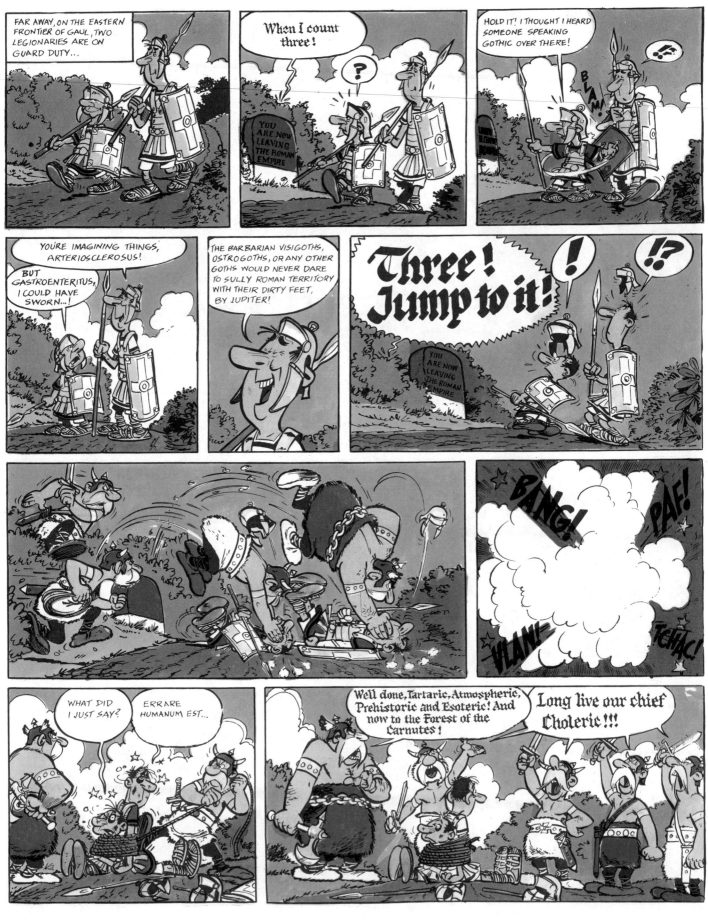

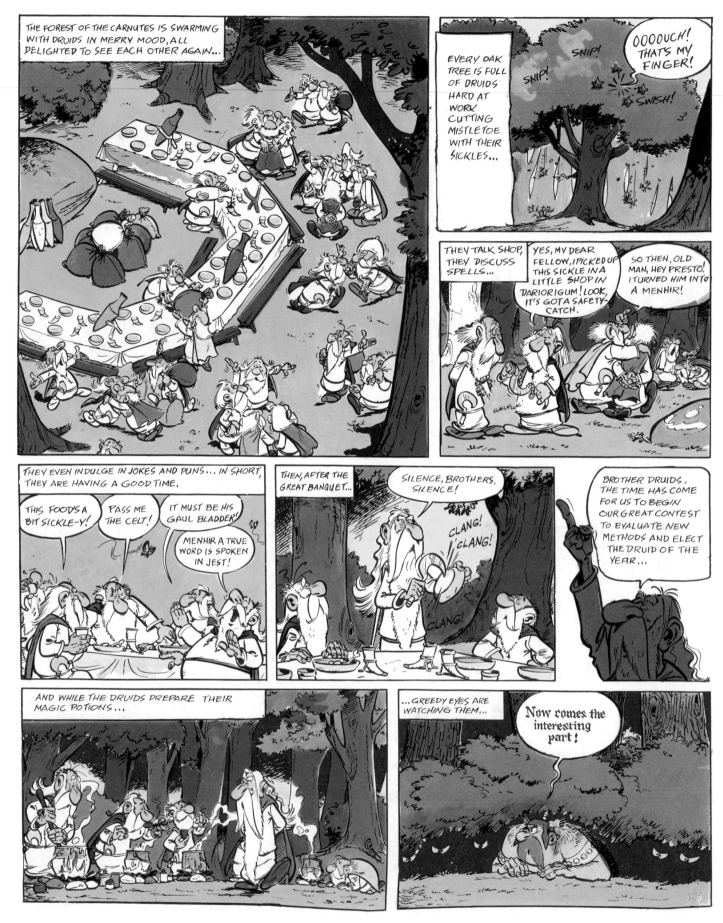

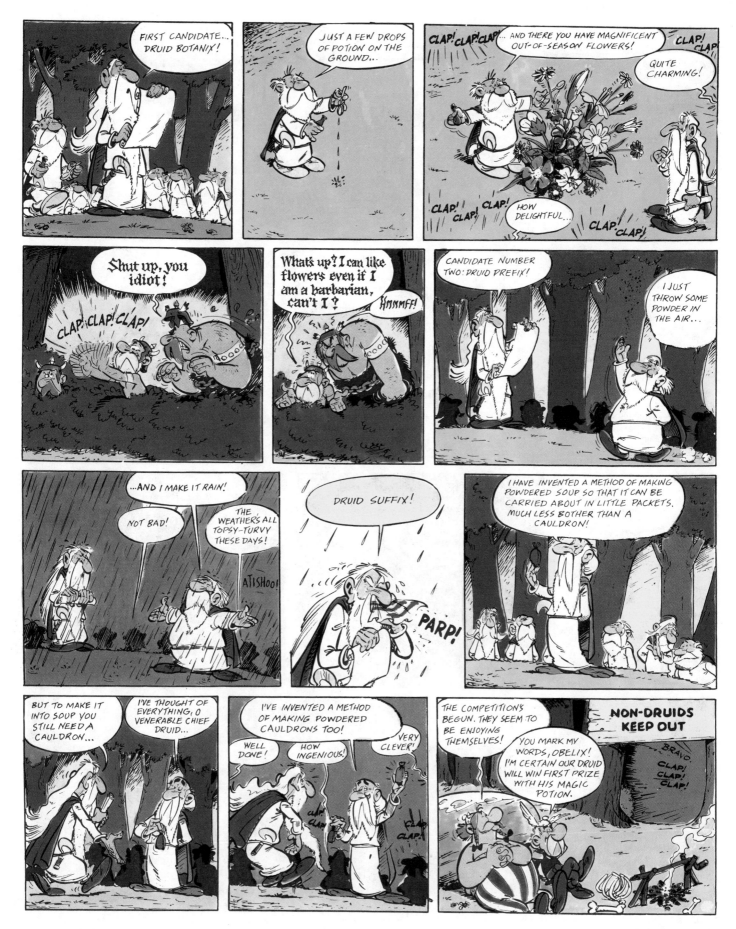

13

AS SOON AS THE ROMANS KNOW THAT THE GOTHS THEY ARE LOOKING FOR ARE DISGUISED AS ROMANS, THERE IS COMPLETE CHAOS... THE ROMANS GO ABOUT CAPTURING ONE ANOTHER...

I'M A ROMAN! I'M A ROMAN! I'M A ROMAN!

GOT YOU, YOU BARBARIAN!

THE UNHAPPY GENERAL CANTANKERUS IS NEARLY OUT OF HIS MIND...

THEY'RE ALL QUITE THICK, AND I'M THEIR LEADER! (SOB! SOB!)

I'M TAKING YOU IN, GOTH!

YOU OFF YOUR HEAD OR SOMETHING?

BUT SOME PEOPLE ARE MAKING THE MOST OF THE SITUATION, FOR INSTANCE, ASTERIX AND OBELIX, WHO HAVE PUT THEIR OWN CLOTHES ON AGAIN...

... AND THE GOTHS, THE ROOT OF ALL THE TROUBLE, WHO ARE PROCEEDING UNEVENTFULLY TOWARDS THEIR OWN COUNTRY OF GERMANIA.

Watch out! The frontier's ahead. We've got to cross it!

A HEAVY RESPONSIBILITY WEIGHS ON THOSE WHO GUARD THE FRONTIER AGAINST FOREIGN INVADERS...

GAUL
ROMAN EMPIRE

Germania

Hey!

HMMM?

GAUL ROMAN EMPIRE

BONG!

Victory is ours! We'll be given a hero's welcome by our own people!

Anything to declare?

22

24

29

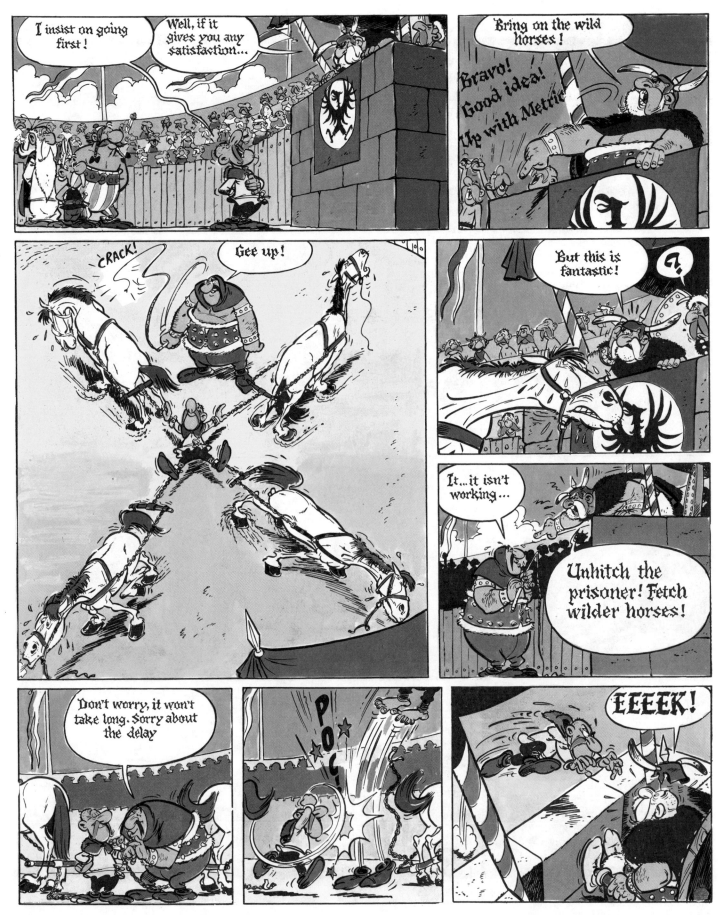

43

44

Metric

Rhetoric

THE ASTERIXIAN WARS
A Tangled Web . . .

The ruse employed by Asterix, Getafix and Obelix succeeded beyond their wildest dreams. After drinking the druid's magic potion, the Goths fought each other tooth and nail. Here is a brief summary to help you follow the history of these famous wars.

The favourite and devastating weapon of the combatants.

Diagram indicating the course of events.

The first victory is won outright by Rhetoric, who, having surprised Metric by an outflanking movement, lets him have it – bonk! – and inflicts a crushing defeat on him. This defeat, however, is only temporary . . .

Rhetoric has no time to celebrate his victory, for, having completed his outflanking movement, he is taken in the rear by his own ally, Lyric. Lyric instantly proclaims himself supreme chief of all the Goths, much to the amusement of the other chiefs . . . .

Who turn out to be right, for Lyric's brother-in-law Satiric lays an ambush for him, pretending to invite him to a family reunion and Lyric falls into the trap. It was upon this occasion that the proposition that blood is thicker than water was first put to the test . . .

Rhetoric goes after Lyric, with the avowed intention of "bashing him up" (archaic), but his rearguard is surprised by Metric's vanguard. Bonk! This manoeuvre is known as the Metric System.

General Electric manages to surprise Euphoric meditating on the conduct of his next few campaigns. Euphoric's morale is distinctly lowered, but he has the last word, with his famous remark, "I'll short-circuit him yet"

While Electric proclaims himself supreme chief of the Goths, to the amusement of all and sundry, it is the turn of Metric's rearguard to be surprised by Rhetoric's vanguard. Bonk! "This is bad for my system," is the comment of the exasperated Metric.

In fact, it is so bad for his system that he allows himself to be surprised by Euphoric. The battle is short and sharp. Euphoric, a wily politician, instantly proclaims himself supreme chief of the Goths. The other supreme chiefs are in fits . . .

Euphoric, much annoyed, sets up camp and decides to sulk. He is surprised by Eccentric, who in his turn is attacked by Lyric, subsequently to be defeated by Electric. Electric is destined to be betrayed by Satiric, who will be beaten by Rhetoric.

Going round a corner, Rhetoric's vanguard bumps into Metric's vanguard. Bonk! Bonk! This battle is famous in the Asterixian wars as the "Battle of the Two Losers" And so the war goes on . . .

MEANWHILE, OUR THREE FRIENDS ARE APPROACHING THE FRONTIER OF GAUL, WITH THEIR MINDS AT REST...

45

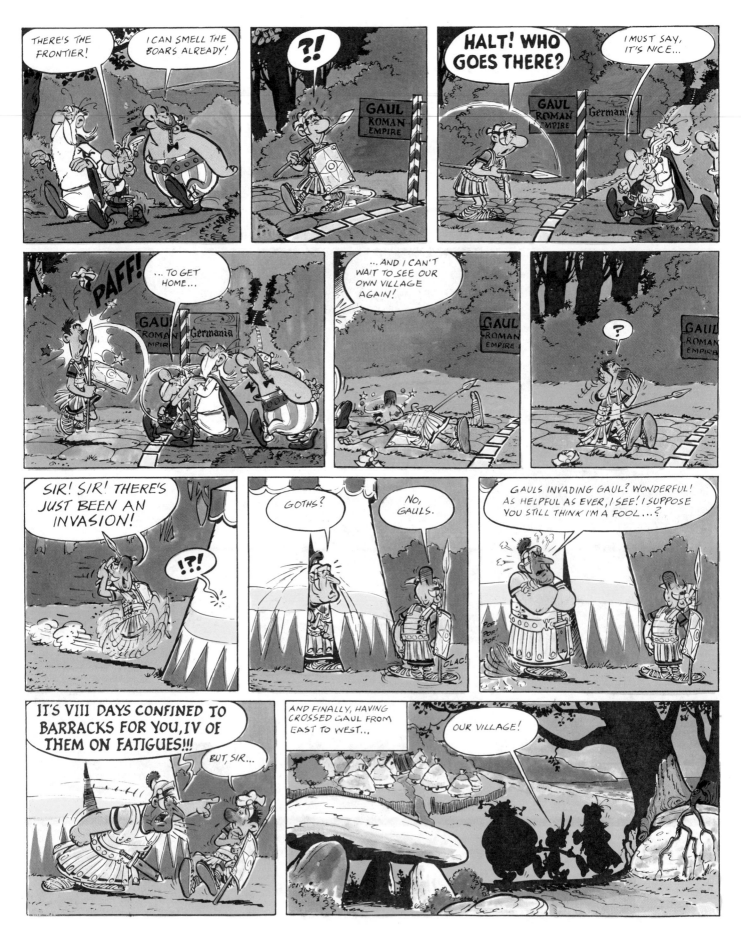